W9-BEP-248

Summertime WALTZ

Summertime WALTZ

Nina Payne

Pictures by Gabi Swiatkowska

FRANCES FOSTER BOOKS
FARRAR, STRAUS AND GIROUX
NEW YORK

To you

—N.P. and G.S.

Lovely the lateness
in summertime darkening.
Dinner is over.
The grownups are talking.
Smell of the water
on pots of geraniums.
Lovely the lateness
in summertime dark.

Outside and inside
is lost in the doorways
. . . forty-nine, ready
or not, here I come!
Moths and mosquitoes
are biting the lampposts.
Outside and inside
is lost at the door.

No one is leaving,
then everyone's running
to look for the ball
as it rolls into morning.
Millicent Tomkins!
Your mother is calling.
No one is leaving,
then everyone's gone.

Lovely the lateness in

summertime darkening

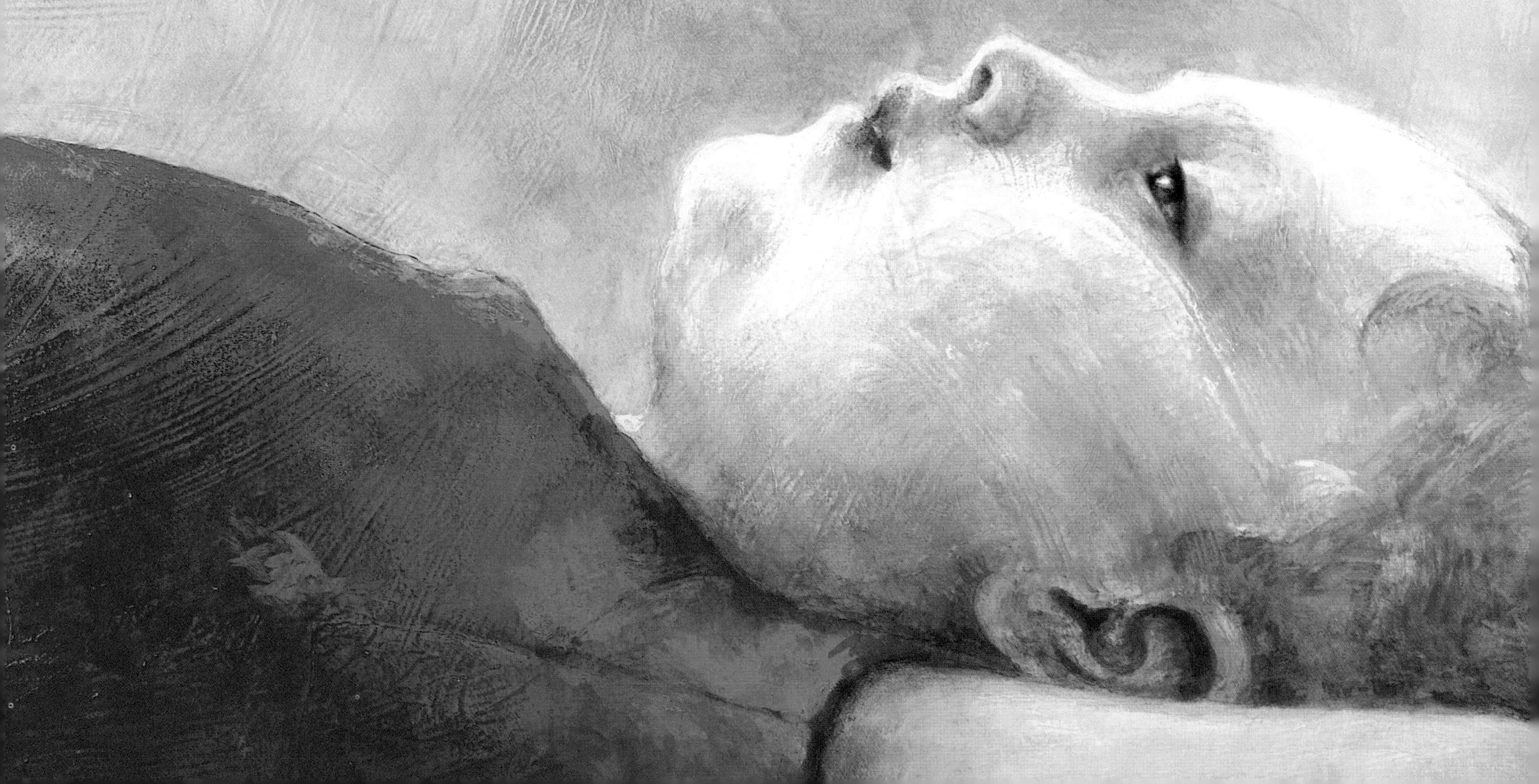

IS

DINNER  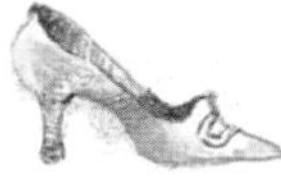 OVER.

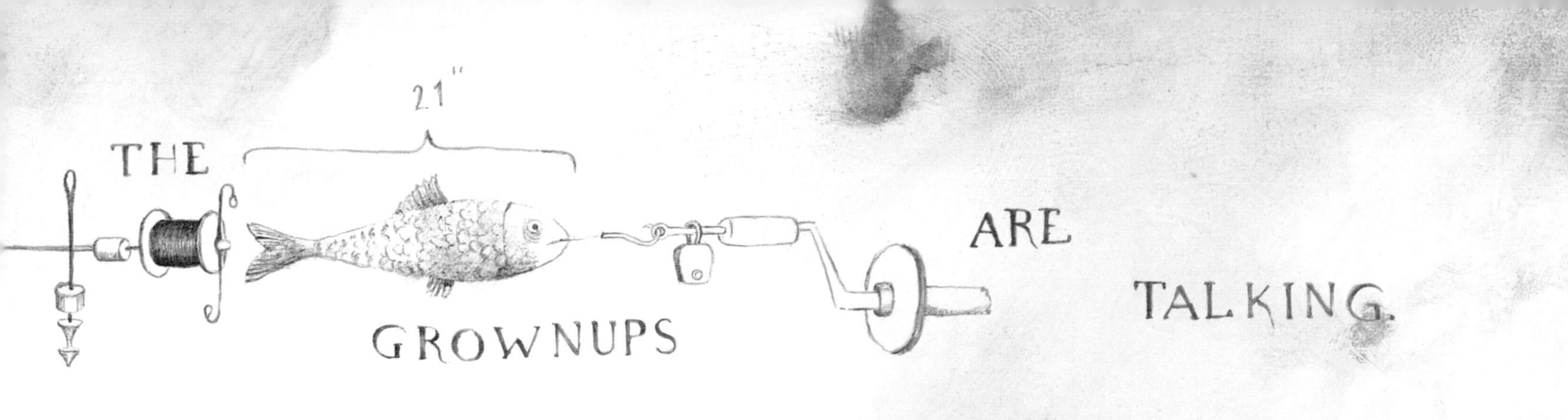
THE
21"
GROWNUPS
ARE
TALKING.

Smell of the

water on

pots of

geraniums

Lovely the lateness

in summertime dark.

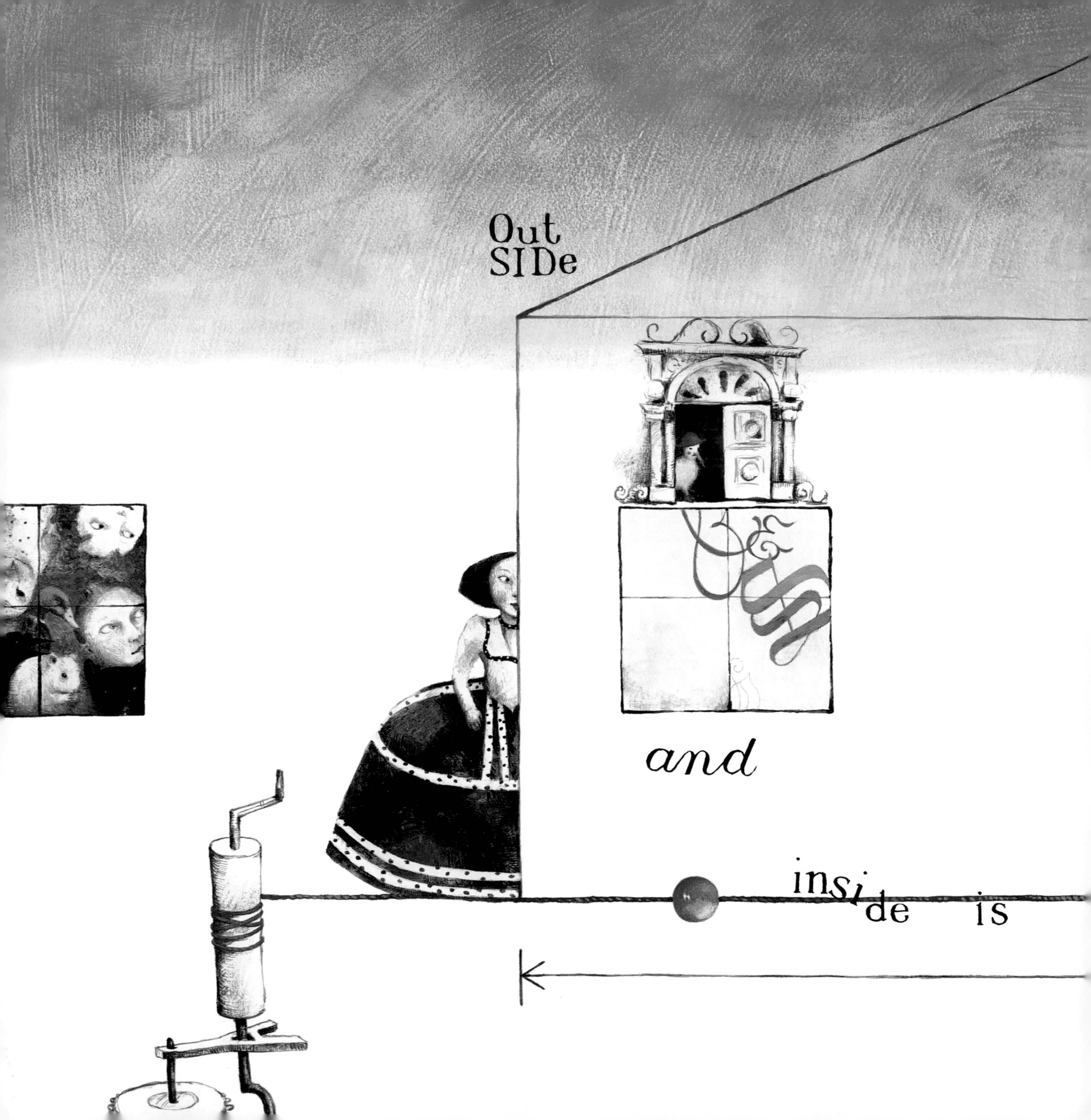
Out
SIDe
and
inside is

lost in the
doorways

17

. . . forty-nine, READY OR NOT, HERE I COME!

2

8

Moths and mosquitoes

aRe Biting the lAmPPostS

outside

and

inside is lost at

the

door.

No
oNE
is
Leaving
then

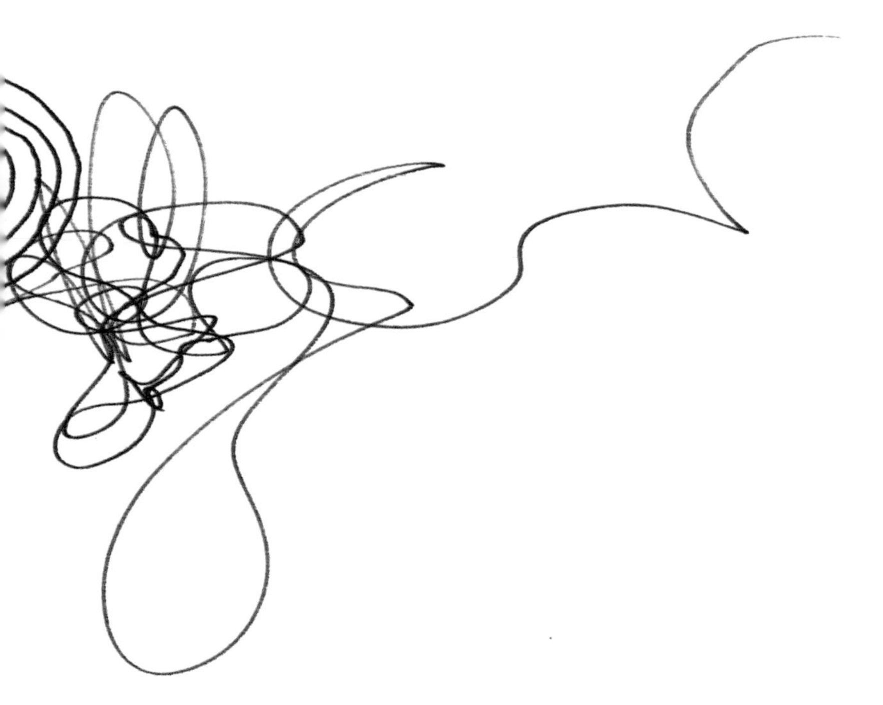

everyone's running

to look for the morning.

ball as it rolls into

millicent Tomkins!

your mother is calling.

no one is leaving.

then everyone's gone.

Distributed in Canada by Douglas & McIntyre Publishing Group
Color separations by Chroma Graphics PTE Ltd.
Printed and bound in the United States of America by Berryville Graphics
Designed by Robbin Gourley and Jay Colvin
First edition, 2005
3 5 7 9 10 8 6 4 2

www.fsgkidsbooks.com

Library of Congress Cataloging-in-Publication Data
Payne, Nina.
Summertime waltz / Nina Payne ; pictures by Gabi Swiatkowska.— 1st ed.
p. cm.
Summary: Illustrations and rhythmic text describe the delights of a summer evening.
ISBN-13: 978-0-374-37291-0
ISBN-10: 0-374-37291-8
[1. Summer—Fiction.] I. Swiatkowska, Gabriela, ill. II. Title.

PZ7.P2966Su 2005
[E]—dc22

2003049246